THE LUXURY NIGHTMARE

PRATIK DAS

ISBN 979-888521946-4

Contents

Acknowledgements

The Luxury Nightmare by Pratik Das, is completely a friction story book, it does not have any connection on any real incident or person. If any connection has been found with any person or with any such incident then it's totally a coincidence.

ABOUT THE AUTHOR :

Pratik Das is well known for his social works across the town. A bong boy from a common middle class family with high ambitions to be the helping hand for needy living beings. Likes the zone of positive people, because he believe learning has no age and sharing knowledge has no limits. Politically aware, like minded and down to earth is his first and foremost priority. Has a huge crush on sports, especially cricket. Crazy fan of Sourav Ganguly (Dada), Biriyani and love dogs more than anything.

Follow Me on Facebook : Pratik

CHAPTER ONE

The Luxury Nightmare

In former times their lived a young boy from a happy family in the heart of the metropolitan City of Joy, Kolkata. Though he grew up from a small town by due to this father's job, he and his mother shifted to Kolkata.

Gourab's mother is a house wife and he has full of dream to do something big in the city, so that his and his parents names gets famous and known to all. As he is not from such a big city and neither he knows the city too well, he get's into difficult situation many instances.

It's just few years ago he completed his studies in M.Sc in Hospitality Management from a well known college in Kolkata. But from his childhood, he never wants to do job, their fore after completing his graduation when everyone in his family forced him to do job, he just pass over their words as if he wants to do more study. But actually he wants to do business and get fame and money for his family and for himself as well.

Now it's almost 4 years passed without any job, and in this 4 years he tried almost 22 types of business and all of them has failed, some of them has failed due to his staffs behaviour with the customers, some of them failed due to lack of his knowledge in the particular business but most of the business ruined due to people cheated on him and took the products or services he is offing without making payment. And he is too bashful to ask for money. But as the days were passing he is getting the pressure, and now it's almost limit-less for him to survive with no money in this situation.

Gourab has a huge pressure for his failure in business and also from his parents who are forcing him to do a job from the beginning as his father is going to retire within few months, but as he has no interest in jobs and now he has no money to start a new business again. Day by day the pressuring is building on him. Although he has a good habit of praying to GOD everyday as taught by his mother from childhood. And during this days his praying to GOD has became more frequently.

But every-time he starts a business it's failed and he became depress. But at this time he is even more depress as he has no money to start a new business and the pressure is squeezing him. He has a dream of a successful businessman and success means to him is money and fames. He only prays for money and fames to GOD. From his childhood he has a dream of big luxury villa, big luxury cars and fame for his name. But now as per the situation demand he needs money to do anything and that makes him frustrated and anger.

After trying all from his side and not getting any path that can take him where he desire, he simply went to the temple in his locality where he and his family use to perform Puja from the time they arrived in Kolkata. He took a lonely place in the temple and seat quietly, so that he could get a good view of GOD from that place but inside he has a burning volcano that's ready to erupt. Now all his anger and frustrating in on GOD, as starting any new business he always pray for success of the business to GOD.

He didn't find any faults of him behind the failure of 22 businesses. Now he directly starts blaming GOD for everything. After an hour the priest closed the doors and ask him to leave the temple as it's already too late. But he didn't moved an inch and asked the priest to leave and closed the temple, but he will not leave the temple until he gets any reply from GOD. As the priest knows him very well and everyone in his locality knows him as a good boy, the priest agreed and ask him to closed the door from outside. Though the priest has closed the main door of the temple. it's not a long time they were living in Kolkata but as he and his family were decent and well-behaved and helpful so everyone like and respect them. And due to that the priest left the temple without closing the main door.

Now due to anger and due to his gullible he is questioning GOD one by one, without caring the time and not controlling over his mouth, as if all the fault is due to GOD and created by GOD. But here in his home as his father is taking sleeping peels due to his health issues, so he slept early but his mother is worried about his son as he doesn't come home late without any reason or without letting them know. Due to worry his mother waiting for him in their balcony and started praying to GOD so that his son come back home soon or even call her from anywhere, as his phone is switch-off from the evening. As the time passes but still her son not came home, now his mother start chanting GOD's name.

But on the other side her son, Gourab still in the temple and still in the same mood and going on questing GOD. It's almost half of the night but still his energy on questing GOD is same. During this time he heard a sound of someone coughing from the other side of the temple. But he didn't react, again he heard the sound of coughing and now he turned back and saw a lady in white and red saree, staring at him. He got confused because it was too late for anyone to present in the temple at that time and mostly confused as he was alone in the temple for last few hours.

With a disoriented face Gourab asked the lady ; "please go mam the temple is closed for today, and also it's too late in the night" politely and turned. After few minutes he saw the lady is still standing, without any reply, and Gourab has to stop and got a bit irked and swell his voice a bit and repeat the same "please go mam the temple is closed for today, and also it's too late in the night", the lady said, I know Gourab, I know everything of everyone. Gourab asked, how do you know my name? in a shocking voice and what you know? The lady reply I told you Gourab, I know everything of everyone, and I know why you are here and what you want?

Now Gourab thought she might be anyone, might be bugler or cheater or might be a group of corrupt people who loots and robbed people. He quickly tries to hide the golden ring that his mother has gifted him on his last birthday. He put his hand inside the pocket and look here and their, to find whether she is alone or she is in a group. But he couldn't find anyone, though it was dark out side the temple as the light on the post near the temple got death from last few days. Now Gourab has no choice and he can't ignore her as it's late in the night and she is alone. So Gourab took a save place infront the temple so that if something wrong happens, he could ran easily. Gourab asked, mam could you tell what you want at this time in the night, in the temple and I heard from my mother that GOD sleeps at night, so if you came here to Pray or to give Puja kindly come tomorrow morning when the temple will open. The lady replied politely, it seems you know everything then why you are here, when your mother told you GOD sleeps at night. Gourab reply, because GOD is not doing right with me. The lady asked, what not right GOD has done with you tell me, though I know everything.

Now after hearing all this from her mouth and that also so confidently she told, that Gourab got muted for few seconds. Because looking at the lady Gourab got a feelings that she can't be a bugler or cheater or a group of corrupt people who loots and robbed people, because she is so polite, so gentle and a smell of purity and holy comes from her surrounding. And now Gourab reply slowly, do you know why am here!! The lady reply politely, Yes my child. Now the curiosity in his mind is on the top floor that how could she knows everything about him, because he doesn't share his failure to anyone without his parents and GOD. So with curiosity he asked may I know who are you ? The lady reply am everything in this world. Am the little bird who sing in the morning, am that little dog who bark at night, am that little child who weep sometimes, am inside everyone and everything.

Gourab amazed and shocked at the same time. Without controlling himself he started crying, and whisper please tell me Ma (GOD) why I became a failure, though I gave my 100% and with all honesty. Ma (GOD) replied, my son can I ask you a question, Gourab replied yes sure Ma (GOD) in weeping voice.

Ma (GOD) asked, how many chop you need to break a stone? Gourab replied, a stone needs many chopped to break into small particles. Ma (GOD) replied yes my son, and in the last chop when it will break into small particles, that doesn't mean you are not giving your 100% from the first chop, but when the time came it break into small particles.

This is life my child, and life is hard but not impossible. If we continue our good work we will get success when our time will come, like the stone break into small particles. Gourab got his answer and feels very exciting and exceptional because Ma (GOD) has come to visit him. So he started thanking Ma (GOD), but Ma (GOD) reply, am not here because you called me, am here because your Ma (Mother) is worried for you as its too late in the night and you have not informed her. Gourab realized his fault and feel sorry for his mother, and quickly switch on his mobile and called his mother. While talking with his mother Gourab realized that Ma (GOD) is about to leave, so he quickly hang-up the phone and asked Ma (GOD), are you leaving ? Ma (GOD) replied; with a smile, I thing you have got your answer. Gourab, yes Ma (GOD), I got my answer but I need something from you, and you have to promise me that you will give it to me.

Ma (GOD) replied, my son I told you before also, am in everything and everywhere in this world. What you want more? Just remember me am with you my son. Gourab; thank you Ma (GOD), but I want you to fulfill my dream that I have seen since, am a child. Because you know everything Ma (GOD), my father is going to retired from his job soon and I have tried 22 business till now but no success yet. All my friends and subordinates have settled their life.

Ma (GOD), to Gourab, you will achieved your success, just continue your good work like before, always remember "Before Time and After Time no one Has Got Anything, When Your Time Will Come You Will Achieve Your Goals". But looking at Gourab face Ma (GOD) told, see that flower plant Gourab inside the temple, you have grown it with the help of the priest. But does the plant gives flower directly or soon you have plant it !! First you plant it, then it grew up, then it produced seeds and then finally it blossom into a beautiful flower. Do you understand my son Ma (GOD) said to Gourab.

Gourab is not in a mood to leave Ma (GOD), as because he has a dream of doing business for name as reputation, frame and money, from his childhood. And at the same time Ma (GOD), is standing infront of him and talking to him, so he want Ma (GOD), to full fill his dream now only. He just constantly appealing to Ma (GOD), to full fill his dream now, as he waited for a long since childhood. After some time Ma (GOD), asked Gourab, tell my son what you want, but before telling me you should keep in mind, that if you are not happy or you face any problem and wants to come back at the present situation then I can't, everything will be your responsibility and you can't blame anyone. Without thinking anything Gourab said, Yes of course; who doesn't want a successful life. And as its my dream to become a successful businessman. Ma (GOD) replied; ok my son, tell me what you want?

Gaurab, I want a successful life, with my only name in the newspaper, when I go from the road everything should be stopped, when I visit any place there should be only me. Everyone should stare at my big and beautiful cars, I should get what I want to eat anytime in my kitchen and all rest of my desire gets completed. Ma (GOD) after looking to Goaurab's face for few second are you sure? You want all this ? Gaurab, with a big Yes to Ma (GOD).

Ma (GOD) replied Ok my son, Tathastu. And Ma (GOD) disappear in the speed of light. Gaurab feels very happy now and thank Ma (GOD) for blessing him and went back to his home.

After visiting his home he saw his mother in a very exhausted manner. Gaurab feels sorry as he kept his mother waiting without saying anything. He quickly hugs her and whisper slowly, everything will be great now within few days. And request his mother to sleep as soon as possible because tomorrow he will tell her many things. Without asking anything his mother took a deep breath and went to sleep so as Gourab.

Next day morning around 6.45 AM suddenly with the brightness of sun light, kissed Gaurab's forehead and he woke up. After waking up he just sit on his bed and start surfing his social media account. And what every he opened he just see himself and himself only, he didn't understand and closed everything and gets down from his bed. And he shocked and put his feet up in the bed again as he saw the floor is not the regular floor of his room, he has a normal floor but now he sees a one-piece marble floor. He rubbed his eyes and started to see his room and he shocked again as everything has been changed and after few minutes he recall what happened last night, and started smiling and gets down from his bed.

While coming to his drawing room he saw his 2 bed room house has been converted into a luxury villa and exactly how he use to dream with numerous rooms. He came to the kitchen and opened the drawers and saw few world famous tea brands and coffee brands, with all his favourite snacks, he tastes few of them and start reading the newspaper, and saw it's only him and his success story in the newspaper. He feels proud and happy for himself and for his parents. Exactly how he use to dream. He quickly called his mother and father by shouting many times, but he got no answer. The he pick his mobile and called them, their phone is switch off. He feels a little bad about where they both gone when their son is so successful. He went out of his luxury villa and saw a big fountain, a tennis court with some imported rackets, a big basket ball lane, a golf course and few imported cars which he always desire.

Now his excitement level goes up double as he saw his villa from out side. It's so big that it can have his full province inside his villa and so beautiful that it might be the 8th wonder of the world, Gourab thinks. And feels too happy for himself and too eager for his parents to show them all this. But unfortunately they were not present at the moment. He started playing tennis all alone but after few times later he gets bored and started calling his friends to invite them in his luxury villa and also to play with him. But every ones phone is switch off, he gets frustrated and walk towards his fridge. And open them and saw the fridge filled with worlds finest alcohols and rare and few filled with costly beers around the world. He gets very excited and start taking a peg of each one, to taste them. After few hours due to Intoxication he fell asleep. Next day morning he woke up a little early before the sun light kissed his forehead.

As he is feeling hangover he went to take bath in his luxury bathroom with different types of natural and imported soaps. After few time he rapped his towel and went to the pool in his terrace and start singing the song his mother use to sing during his childhood, while bathing him. He is missing his parents, specially his mother but acts like why should he call as their phone is switch off, not his. And start playing in the pool with water and clicking photos to upload in his social media.

After few times later he tried to post those pictures on his social media accounts, but he can't whatever social media account he opened he just seeing him only and nothing. And this is what he always desire. As the day progresses he is feeling hot in his terrace pool. So he left the pool to have food for himself. He went to the 2000sq ft kitchen and start eating one by one every delicious items. Suddenly from the window he saw the luxury cars in his garden. He quickly left everything and dressed like a groom to go out with one of the luxury car. He started the car by his figure print and the feels he gets is just priceless.

He has a dream for luxury cars from childhood. But he never thought of so many luxury cars at a time. Now he started driving towards the city and thought everyone will stare at his car, so he put the music loud so that he gets more attention. After few times later he noticed the roads are all empty, he couldn't see any one, not even a street dog or a cat. He gets confused and started driving faster so that people from their houses notice him. But he was wrong, there is no one to see neither his car nor him. He then came back to his luxury villa and start drinking the finest alcohol, foods and also all the nuts available in his villa, due to frustration. Now as the time passes he is getting bored and frustrated as because he is so alone.

He switch on the television and just see him on all the channels and nothing at all. He switch on his social media accounts and see just him and nothing at all. He took the newspaper and see the newspaper is full with his story and him only and nothing else. He tried to call his friends, relatives and parents but nothing positive happens, every ones phone is switch off. His frustration levels goes up and he got asleep as there is no one with whom he can share or talk.

Days passing like he is swimming The English Channel all alone. And day by day he is becoming more and more frustrated and irritated. When ever and what ever he do he feels too alone. Now day by day he feels probably like the last man on earth.

Few days later he went to the shopping mall, he does shopping many expensive items for himself and for his parents but there is no one to whom he give them or share. He buys many expensive items for his mother, but feels so unlucky as he couldn't give her neither could talk with them as their phone is switch off. Event in the shopping mall is all empty, he bought and pay online and took the receipt all alone, even there is no one at the outside door of the shopping mall to check any fraud case.

Day by day he is just becoming ugly with huge hairs over his head and long bread with moustache all over his face. Its seems like he has forgotten how to leave though he has everything now. Like this time passes and he's getting more and more frustrated, Gourab just getting foil over his life. He couldn't find any way nor anyone in the world and started feeling like The Last Man on Earth. Now he has everything, every luxury of his life but he doesn't have anyone beside him. Gourab remember and recall everything that happened that night in the temple. He recall what he has asked from Ma (GOD) and now he realized that it is his fault. He has always asked a life like this from his childhood, he ask for luxury cars, big luxury villa with all facility in it, he asked for unlimited money, he asked for name and fame so that it's only him on everywhere and today he got everything but didn't ask for peace, happiness and family. Though he loved his parents but while asking to Ma (GOD) he didn't utter their name once. And Ma (GOD) gave him what he wants always. And he also know that Ma (GOD) has warn him ask him to think because once he get everything Ma (GOD) will not help him to go to his previous life. By thinking all this few more days went away, but he couldn't find any solution. Now he just looks like a tribal of Africa who has a luxury villa, richest alcohols, finest cars and all the luxury items of the world. That night Gourab is thinking and enjoying his pasted childhood days, on every birthdays of his, he has a picture with his mother starting from the beginning. First on her laps, then holding her hand tightly with a shaking legs of his and slowly he grew up and crossed his mother in height, and he remember that his mother use to say him, "Slowly and Steady Wins the Race". And remembering the pictures and tries to understood the meaning of his mother's words.

Next day morning he woke up a bit late as last night he sleeps late. But as soon as he wakeup, he knows that only Ma (GOD) can only help him out from here. So he started to pray to Ma (GOD). Morning , afternoon, evening and night he has just one thing to utter in his mouth Ma (GOD) "Save Me, Save Me From Here".

But days passed, months passed he is still their without no one. He feels so unlucky for his parents and disgusting for himself that he always cry like a new born baby. He remember the golden days when he lived with his parents, neighbor and friends. Then he doesn't have a luxury life like this but he has mental support, sharing happiness and will power. He recall how he has failed in the passed 22 business and still his parents has full support and determination that he can do and he will do. He recall how his mother has managed his father so that he could do business instead job. He recall how his mother always waits for him without having food, whenever he used to come late home. He recall how his father use to run their family so hardly although he has just few days left in his job. He also recall what Ma (GOD) has said, "Before Time, After Time No One Will Get, What They Want", they will get when their time will come. He recall everything and this makes him more unhappy and he burst into tears.

Gaurab has a huge mango tree in his garden, beside the water fountain, now the tree is full of small mangoes and he liked mangos more than any other. He loves mangoes so much that during mangos season he eats mango during breakfast, lunch and even in dinner. A dish of mango is must, and for that his mother always quotes him as he use to eat too many mangoes. He remember that all words of his mother and break into tears.

He couldn't find any way to go back to his previously life, he thinks that if at this time he's in his past life then he must saying unpleasant words to GOD for his fail in business and must have demand a luxury life like this, and simper.

Now he realized how big mistake he did by asking a luxury, famous and rich life like this, instead he must ask for her Blessings, Power to fight all situation, a healthy life and progress in work. He understood that skipping stairs is not success at all, for a time being he feels good but after that he understand his mistake. Time passes like flowing water from a broken damp. Now the mangoes become big in size and also few changed color from green to Vivid yellow. And as he loves mangos too much he tries to pick them from the tree by throwing stones on them. He got few but from the beginning he is aiming a big juice mango. But it's doesn't picket up from the tree nor fall and got down though he hit it with stones many times. As he got few mangoes so he didn't try again and quickly ran towards his kitchen and cut them into pieces and start eating them. While eating them he remember his childhood days when he and Bikram his best friend used to pick mangoes by throwing stones to them, and eat them without cutting by just pressing them with their small hand until the mangos turned into thin liquid.

Well now Bikram is a Government Job holder and lived out of Kolkata for his job, they haven't meet each other for a long time, but he knows if Bikram knows his condition, he must have done something to help him out from this situation. Gourab also remember how Bikram has helped him by funding a amount of Rs 57,000/- during his export import business, with one condition that once his business become successful he must give a treat to Bikram. And all this makes him feel sad and alone again.

Next day morning he again started throwing stones to that big juice mango, after hitting so many stones, still it didn't came down. With frustration over his head he took one of his luxury car and went away. For the next few days he didn't goes to the garden as seeing that mangos he gets frustrated.

Suddenly one day while praying to Ma (GOD) he heard a sound in his garden. He quickly ran into the garden and saw that big juicy mango has fallen alone though he has not thrown stones for last few days. Gourab got stunned and tuned like a statue for a minute, and then burst into tears.

Because he remember what Ma (GOD) has said to him that night, that " before time, after time, no one has got nothing, everyone will shine when their time will come". While doing business he has given his 100% but still he didn't got success, the same way he has thrown many stones to that mango, but it didn't came to his hand. But now the mango is fully ripe and ready to eat.

Gaurab understood his faults and mistakes and started crying loudly. That whole day he just cried and hope to get back to his home and starts a new journey of his life, but he couldn't. Next day morning when he woke up he saw ants all over his room, as his room and his luxury villa is full of eaten and rotten foods. He throws away few from his body but still there are some as he turned into dirty fellow.

As there is no one with him he got a friend, he talked with them, share all his experiences and his mistakes. And learn how team player they are, while Gaurab says so many things to them he noticed, the ants doesn't listen to him at all and many time he tries to break their concentration and convert their attention towards him. He saw the ants just have a huge focus on their work and it's the same as it is in the morning, evening or even in the night. They just busy carrying the food to their destination, and so much focused that Gaurab gives a wind blow from his mouth, few got misplaced but again came back to same place, same work with same concentration. He changed the food direction and the ants also changed their direction too. He put few drops of water to shift their focus, but the ants also changed their line and continue their work.

That day he learn a big lesson from the ants, that "Working in team with focus makes Success." Thinking about all this he planed for next what he is going to do and how he will run his business, but for that he needs to get back to his normal previous life. With a big dissatisfaction in his heart he goes to sleep and just begging to Ma (GOD) so that he could gets back to his normal life and this time he just need blessings, by chanting all this slowly he goes to sleep.

Next day morning he realized a hand over his forehead and quickly open his eyes, he saw his mother calling him. He looked in a shocking manner to her and turned his eyes all over his room, he just can't believe that he came back to his normal life. He tightly hug his mother and slowly whisper "am sorry". His mother said, you must be because your friend Bikram is waiting for you from last 1hour as he came from so far and after so many days. Gaurab's shocked again, and said after so many days later I saw you, our home and came back to my previous life and in bonus I got Bikram to meet after so many days, and smiled by looking into his mother's face. Now his mother shocked a bit as well, and replied, what are you saying? Last night due to depression you goes to sleep late so I didn't call you in the morning, but it's already going to be afternoon. Gaurab asked his mother, didn't am missing for few months or may be a year? A big no over her mouth and looking amazed to Gourab face and try to understand his words. He quickly ran towards the mirror and saw himself, he saw the same Gourab and not in that disaster look. His mother said, you must have seen a dream, don't worry. Again Gaurab got shocked, and whisper Dream..!!

He went out from his room in search of his father and started calling him, his mother reply; your father went to bank in the morning for some banking work. He took his sleepers in his hand and quickly ran out of his house, while going out he saw Bikram was waiting for him; Gaurab said, Bikram just wait am coming, I have to say many things. And ran towards the temple, and now he realized he has seen a dream and through that dream Ma (GOD) has given him the best lesson. He prayed to Ma (GOD) and remember each and everything that happens to him in his luxury villa, he thank Ma (GOD) and promised that he will work very hard and he will get success with the blessings of his parents and Ma (GOD).

After paying to Ma (GOD) Gourab feels like getting a new life from Ma (GOD) and went back to his home, thinking about last night and feeling sorry for his words he said in the temple. Coming back to his home he said sorry to Bikram as he was waiting for such a long time. He quickly called Bikram and his mother to his room and started saying each and everything that he did and whatever has happen to him, though it was a dream but he realized his faults and mistakes.

After listing everything Bikram said Happy Birthday my Friend. Gaurab reply today is not my birthday, you know that Bikram! Bikram smiled and replied yes I knew but thanks to Ma (GOD) you have seen the reality of life that money can't makes you happy, but money is an important part of our life. So today with the blessings of Ma(GOD) you have took a rebirth so am wishing you happy birthday. Now the both are laughing and thanking Ma(GOD). But his mother has not said anything just gave a smile and hug Gourab tightly and went to the kitchen.

In between Bikram said I came here for a proposal and a request. Gaurab said yes please my dear friend tell what can I do for you? Bikram as you know am living out of Kolkata due to my job but from next month I will be in Kolkata as my transfer is approved. Gaurab hugs him with happiness and said thank you now I will be not alone. Bikram said, there is a request also and I don't want to hear any negative reply from you. Gaurab said what it is? Bikram said as I will be now in Kolkata so am thinking to start a restaurants and I want you my friend as a partner of 50%. You don't have to invest a single penny except your business ideas and good will.

Gaurab burst into happiness and hugs Bikram tightly and said, before also you have given me Rs 57,000/- for my business and neither I have given you back the money nor I can give you the treat as it's failed. Bikram smiled and replied I have given that money in one condition that once you got success in business you must give me a treat.

But don't worry this time you will give me two treats, is that makes you happy now? Gaurab smiled and reply softly thank you Bikram, for standing beside me and gets emotional. Without saying anything Bikram gave a cheque of

Rs 1,00,000/- and ask Gourab to start the preparation of their restaurant and this time he, his parents and Ma (GOD) is with him, so no need to worry just focus and start working.

Tears in his eyes Gourab remember a famous quotes by Ma Sarada – "He who will pray to GOD eagerly will see him."